THOUGHTFULNESS THINKING

Positive Thinking

A Starfish Book

Vicky Bureau
M.S., School Counseling

SEAHORSE PUBLISHING

Teaching Tips for Caregivers:

As a caregiver, you can help your child succeed in school by giving them a strong foundation in language and literacy skills and a desire to learn to read.

This book helps children grow by letting them practice reading skills.

Reading for pleasure and interest will help your child to develop reading skills and will give your child the opportunity to practice these skills in meaningful ways.

- Encourage your child to read on her own at home
- Encourage your child to practice reading aloud
- Encourage activities that require reading
- Establish a reading time
- Talk with your child
- Give your child writing materials

Teaching Tips for Teachers:

Research shows that one of the best ways for students to learn a new topic is to read about it.

Before Reading

- Read the "Words to Know" and discuss the meaning of each word.
- Read the back cover to see what the book is about.

During Reading

- When a student gets to a word that is unknown, ask them to look at the rest of the sentence to find clues to help with the meaning of the unknown word.
- Ask the student to write down any pages of the book that were confusing to them.

After Reading

- Discuss the main idea of the book.
- Ask students to give one detail that they learned in the book by showing a text dependent answer from the book.

TABLE OF CONTENTS

Positivity: Do You Have It?

Do clouds make you worry about rain? Or do they make you feel excited about rainbows?

And what if it does rain? Will wet socks make you feel annoyed? Or will you throw them off and dance in the puddles?

Sometimes, it's hard to see the bright side.

Sometimes, we don't even want to try.

But **positive** thinking helps us try harder, push farther, and smile more often!

You may not see it now, but it's actually harder to fail than it is to succeed!

Well, at least when it comes to
your **attitude**.

In other words, it’s okay to have doubt...

...as long as you keep hope!

It's okay to feel unsure...

...as long as you believe it will get better!

Positivity: What Does It Mean?

Will you try a new sport during gym or recess?

Will you make a new friend when your seat is changed at lunch?

Positivity means being able to see the bright side, even when things seem dark. It means seeing the good stuff that is behind the bad stuff.

Sometimes, the good stuff is hiding.

Sometimes, you have to look really hard or dig really deep to find it.

But positivity is always around.
You just need to believe it's there!

Look over here, or behind there, or under this, or over that.

Look within YOU!

Positivity: How Can You Build Yours?

You can learn more about yourself! Want to know how?

For every **negative** thing you can see, think about the positive thing you can find.

What Would You Do?

Your best friend is absent today. Do you make a new friend, or sit alone?

Your schoolwork seems too hard. Do you ask for help, or give up?

The cafeteria runs out of chicken nuggets. Do you try something new, or eat nothing?

Let's review your answers!

Making a new friend can seem scary, but meeting someone unfamiliar can help to build **confidence**!

Learning new things can be frustrating, but all things are difficult before they are easy!

Trying new things can seem scary (almost as scary as the Meatloaf Surprise in the cafeteria). But you never know, you just might like it!

Words to Know

attitude (AT-i-tood): a person's way of thinking or feeling

confidence (KAHN-fuh-dens): a belief that you can succeed

negative (NEG-uh-tiv): not positive; unfavorable or disagreeable; not hopeful or optimistic

positive (PAH-zuh-tiv): not negative; favorable or agreeable; hopeful or optimistic

positivity (PAH-zuh-ti-vi-tee): thinking in a hopeful, happy way

Index

Comprehension Questions

1. How can you show positivity even when things seem hard or difficult?

2. What are some things you can do to help you think more positively?

3. How does a person's attitude affect their positivity?

4. What does it mean to be positive? What does it mean to be negative?

About the Author

Vicky Bureau was born in Longueuil, Quebec, and was raised in South Florida. As a teacher, she developed a passion for the social and emotional growth of her students and later transitioned into the area of child and adolescent psychology after earning her master's degree in school counseling. In addition to working with children, Vicky loves to be surrounded by animals and nature. She lives in Fort Lauderdale with her family: Billy, Khloe, M.J., and Max; her three cats, Alley, Baguette, and Salem; and her dog, Boomer.

Written by: Vicky Bureau
Design by: Under the Oaks Media
Editor: Kim Thompson

Photographs/Shutterstock: Benjavisa Rvangvaree: cover, p. 1; S.Borisov: p. 4-5; Tina Bilankov: p. 5a; Marc Kirby: p. 5b; Dragon Images: p. 6; narikan: p. 7; Mikael Damkier: p. 8; aleks333: p. 9; Asier Romero: p. 10; New Arfica: p. 11, 17a; Monkey Business Images: p. 13, 17c; Kiefer Pix: p. 14-15; spass: p. 16a; ESBProfessional; p. 16b; SOKStudio: 17b; Svitlana Bezuhlova: p. 19

Library of Congress PCN Data
Positive Thinking / Vicky Bureau
Thoughtfulness Thinking
ISBN 978-1-63897-094-1 (hard cover)
ISBN 978-1-63897-180-1 (paperback)
ISBN 978-1-63897-266-2 (EPUB)
ISBN 978-1-63897-352-2 (eBook)
Library of Congress Control Number: 2021945237

Printed in the United States of America.

Seahorse Publishing Company
www.seahorsepub.com

Published in the United States
Seahorse Publishing
PO Box 771325
Coral Springs, FL 33077

SEAHORSE PUBLISHING